Quantum Pulse

Quantum Pulse

TALES FROM THE ETHERIC FIELD

Ria Bonneamie

REGENT PRESS
Berkeley, California

Copyright © 2021 by Ria Bonneamie

[Paperback]
ISBN 10:1-58790-662-7
ISBN 13: 978-1-58790-662-6
Library of Congress Control Number: *forthcoming*

The persons and events in this book are fictional. Names and places have no relevance to any real facts. Any coincidence should be examined thoroughly for cosmic consequences. Canines and other domesticated creatures must be respected, for initially they are innocent, until transformed by humans.

Manufactured in the U.S.A.
REGENT PRESS
Berkeley, California
www.regentpress.net

*Quantum Pulse is dedicated to all my past, present
and future soul mates, my inner family,
my true friends who have helped me thrive
and experience this current lifetime.*

> "Spirit is the life, Mind is the builder,
> and Body is the result."
> EDGAR CAYCE

> "The decision between past, present and future is
> only a stubborn persistent illusion."
> ALBERT EINSTEIN

> "The biggest frontier opens up in front of us, and
> rather than
> be afraid of it, we should go forward with
> courage."
> LINDA MOULTON HOWE

> "Man is crazy. He worships an invisible God, and
> destroys a visible nature, unconscious
> that the Nature he destroys is the God
> he holds in reverence."
> HUBERT REEVES

Table of Contents

3 am
11

Four Wings
29

One Lonely Beach
51

The Road Runner
61

Three Gran Pueblo Lives
69

A Division of Two
81

Three Stone Masons
85

3 AM

In the dream, he was walking away from a large stream, a gushing brown flood, filled with tree snags and rolling boulders. The river was jumping out of its banks, chasing him, trying to grasp his feet. He ran. The water was still rising, roiling noisily behind him. He ran faster. There was a little dry hill to his left. He sprinted to it, dead shrubs whipping his pants legs. He was out of breath, but kept moving up toward the ponderosa trees. His lungs were hurting, his arms were cramping, his shoes were filled with soft mud. He stopped and looked back. The stream was carving a path toward him, following him uphill.

That made no sense, water running uphill as in an Escher drawing. He woke up, drenched in sweat in his large bed. He was glad his girlfriend had not spent the night. He may even have screamed during the nightmare, but could not remember. He would not have wanted her to hear that.

As the night's fog slowly lifted from his brain, he recollected that he had angered his friend two days earlier by not attending her show. For the last couple of months, she had worked hard on her lines for a play by a local artist. It had sounded like a stupid love story, with continuous drama and discussions about whether the partners should seek others while staying married. Was she trying to tell him something? The whole cast in the play was local, mostly friends of hers, no one there he really knew. He had never cared for any of her self-centered friends. And she only cared about how she looked. She was very pretty, but shallow. He would not miss her too long.

That evening he had gone drinking with some of his workmates. And he had done it again last night. He may have drunk too much this time. Drowning his sorrow in a way. She had told him she did not want to see him again, ever. Was that what the dream was about? He did not remember much about that day, except that his best buddy had told him: "No worry, man. You have a good job, your own place, a nice car, and you're a good looking Latino. You'll have no problem finding another girl." That had cheered him up, and he recalled downing another half dozen tequila shots.

~~~

After work the next day, he went grocery shopping, then straight home. No bar tonight. He fixed his favorite meal: a red chile enchilada. He drank just one beer while watching an action movie with plenty of nudity, sex and violence. He showered after only one mezcal nightcap, smooth and tasty. Then he went straight to bed.

The land was dry, a few mesquite shrubs, lots

of snake-broom weeds, lizards and bugs dancing in the sunlight. He was not sure of where he was. Must have driven outside town a few miles. As he walked on a cow trail, he looked up at the turquoise blue sky. Dark voluminous clouds threatened on the West side, coloring the horizon a dark purple. They seemed to be moving to the North. He tripped over a small hole. With a few quick steps, he caught himself before falling. But at once, the clouds were moving overhead at a rapid pace. He turned around, back to where he came from, not wanting to get caught in a downpour. The dark, almost black clouds were moving in. They hovered above him and seemed to move downward. If he kept on walking, the fog from these clouds would swallow him. He would not be able to see the trail. He ran, hoping the car was not parked too far. While looking up at the clouds, he fell into a deep sinkhole he hadn't noticed on his way in. He tried to claw at the walls of dirt as he plunged to the bottom, but it was too far to reach. He thought that he would not be found for a while, he may very well die in this hell hole. He did not remember telling anyone about going for a walk. He did not know where he was, or where he had parked his car, or even which day of the week it was. Wasn't he supposed to go to work today? He reached into his back pocket for his phone, and instead pulled up a small book: 'Reptiles of the Southwest'. The picture of a horny toad was on the front cover. The short lizard opened its mouth and started talking to him in a raspy voice.

"Relax! Someone will come soon. Don't worry." He quickly tossed the book aside and woke up.

What had he done this time? Just a real hot enchilada, a beer and a shot of mezcal. It was only three in the morning. Before he fell back asleep, he decided that after work, he'd talk to his weird neighbor who was into dreams and other esoteric shit like that.

~~~

On his way home, after grabbing a fast food meal and a sweet soda, he knocked on the door across his landing. The guy did not even have a ringer, just a peeping hole at eye level. A full minute passed before the neighbor opened the door. The place reeked of marijuana. There were pictures of Buddha, of old people wearing orange dresses, little statues of elephant-men, multiple-arms dancing gods, and all kinds of other stuff he had no idea what they were.

"Hey, sorry to bother you so late. I was wondering if you could help me." He was invited in, and offered a pull off a large hookah that stood on a round table in the middle of the room. Oh well, when in Rome . . .

After a while, feeling a little blurry and out of place, he recounted his last two dreams. The pony-tailed freak combed his long grey beard with his fingers, his eyes closed. Last year, he had told him how when he was young, he spent an enlightening year in India at the foot of some guru he could barely understand. So, that made him a better person? Anyway, if the weirdo could explain his dream that would make this visit worthwhile. Finally the guy opened his eyes and told him that he had lost something big and was drowning in his sorrow. And also that he was worried about changes and loss. And that maybe he was lazy about altering things around him.

Kind of vague. It felt like a waste of time. He went home next door and suddenly felt very tired. The dope probably, he thought. He brushed his teeth, did not feel like a shower. He took his shoes and pants off, and slammed into bed, soon in a deep sleep.

The moon was just rising, full tonight, and throwing shadows across the wall. He watched the play of light and dark, wondering if there were clouds passing in front of the moon. It could also be from the geometric designs of his semi-transparent drapes, softly flowing in the breeze from the open window. One shape looked like a grey snake, undulating in slow motion. Then taking a more substantial form, its mouth opened wide, showing needle-like teeth. Its forked tongue darted towards him. He hated snakes. They repulsed him, making him feel inferior and vulnerable. Out of the grey background, the snake took on colors. Brown and green. It grew in size as it moved closer to him, to his face, until it was staring right at him with its golden, slitted eyes, its head as big as his. As its thin, red tongue flickered against his mouth, he recoiled. But the snake was wrapping itself around his torso, constricting him, encircling his neck, choking him. He could not breathe.

He woke up in a panic, the sheets were wrapped around his neck, cutting off his airway. It was three am, and he was sweating in the cool night. His shirt and the sheets were drenched in sweat. While he showered off the stink of the night, he thought: That was it. He was never again going to smoke with the freak next door. What else did he put in his pipe? Some kind of mind-twister?

~~~

While eating his lunch, he called his dad. It took a while for the nursing home attendant to connect him. His father had been a heavy equipment operator for twenty years, before he had an accident that had crushed both of his legs. He had let go of his mind when he realized he would not be able to work any longer. The company was paying for his care, but the dementia was getting worse with every passing day. He was glad for the days his dad could remember him.

"It's me. How are you today?"

"Still worthless. Got people taking care of me, you know, all the time now. I don't do anything but sit and watch soap operas on TV with other zombies. How are you?"

"I'm OK. The job's the same. No complaints. Glad it's the week-end... My girlfriend left me. I guess we wanted different things, so it was bound to happen. Listen Dad, I've been having these nightmares, almost every night. Did you have bad dreams, when you were working or after the accident?"

"What kind of bad dreams, son?"

"Last night there was a boa constrictor chocking me. I don't know what that's about."

"A big snake? That's your dick. You don't use your dick enough. Get yourself a woman. That will cure it!"

That did not help at all. Besides his father only heard part of what he told him, like always. The rest went way over his head. He was glad that at least he had recognized him.

~~~

He thought he would not drink any alcohol or smoke dope that night. No spicy food either. Maybe that would make a difference with the nightmares. In the afternoon, he went to the gym and lifted weights for an hour. Maybe if he got really tired before falling asleep, he would not have these spooky dreams.

He took a long, hot shower. His body was tired, but his mind was reeling. Maybe he was starting to have dementia, or brain cancer, or he was going crazy? Or maybe his dad was right and he was low in some nutrient, like testosterone or some other shit like that. He was not worried about his job, or loosing his girlfriend. She was a pain in the ass with her demands all the time. She had been great at first, until she kept wanting more and more of him. He did not need her. Good riddance.

The wide street was well illuminated. He checked his pockets for his keys. He remembered that he had locked the car. He always parked under one of those big street lights to make it harder for anyone to steal it, even if that was a block away. Both sidewalks were filled with people that night. Must be something going on, for so many walking around on a weekday. At first, he was following the crowd, stuck in the middle of it. He must have parked further from his apartment than he remembered. At once, in unison, everyone turned around and faced him, coming right at him. They were all looking forward, but did not seem to see him, as if he did not exist. The guy in front had both arms extended, palms out, and shoved him hard on the center of his chest. He fell on his back, like a bug, waving his legs trying to get right side up. The following mass walked over him, trampling him ceaselessly. He was invisible and there were hundreds of them. He tried rolling over, but that did not help. He rolled back thinking that if he faced them, at least he would see them coming. The very last one got on his hands and knees. Finally someone who would acknowledge him. But no, the guy just crawled over him, digging his fingers into his eyes. He was blinded, but his sense of smell was increased. This last guy smelled like some dead animal, freshly dug out of the ground. Disgusting. He needed to puke.

That's what woke him up. He coughed, trying to get rid of the dream's stink. He turned on the light. Three AM. What was that about? He should find someone who would understand him, maybe he needed to see a shrink.

~~~

That afternoon, five PM took forever to get there. He could not wait to be done with work. A block away, there was a bar where the local lawyers hung out. In particular, he had noticed this intriguing girl. She would sit by the last window, looking out, watching the pedestrians go by as if waiting for someone. He looked inside. Yes, she was at her regular table.

The place was crowded and loud. The bar was filled with white-collars in dark blue or grey suits. At work, he did not have to meet and greet customers, just sit behind a desk and talk on the phone. He felt out of place, just wearing a casual jacket over blue jeans. He walked to the back, toward her table, the only empty seat in the whole place. "Mind if I sit down. It's pretty crowded here today." She nodded her head. He asked: "Hey, are you waiting for anyone?" "No, just you, I guess," she answered with a nice smile. A long black braid and tortoise-shell glasses hiding light blue eyes. Nice face, but she dressed funny: a black pin-striped vest over a yellow, flowery blouse and wide-legged, blue linen pants nobody wore anymore. On her feet, Birkenstock sandals. Different from this crowd, but definitely friendlier.

They exchanges niceties, ordered drinks and talked some more. She was a junior lawyer, but so far never practiced in court. She mostly did research. Boring, but it's a living. He answered that he was an IT support specialist, troubleshooting hardware problems, setting up new systems, updating software. Mostly boring too, but he knew his field well. He liked it and it paid well.

A lull in the conversation, while they drank and ordered another round. He felt he could talk to her on a more personal level. "Hey! On a completely different subject, what do you know about dreams?" She stared at him for a while, and then answered by explaining sleep and dream cycles: the four stages, which lasted an hour and a half to two hours, then started again, until one woke up. She also explained how the last stage was when one had an actual dream, with faster heart and breath rates and REMs, or rapid eyes movements. Everybody dreams, but remember their dreams only when waking up during or immediately after having them.

That was interesting. He told her about his three AM wake-ups for the last few nights. Must be three to four hours of sleep or two sleep cycles, as she called them. Then, he asked her if she wanted to have dinner next door, at the Italian semi-fast food. She agreed.

After the meal, she mentioned how nightmares

were usually about unexplained matters, worries and fears. He did not want to share his dreams. Dicks and zombies! They might reveal too much about him. She commented that if someone did not understand or resolve the meaning of their dream, these may continue for a while, the next one picking up the thread of the last remembered one.

She asked him if he would meet her tomorrow, after work, at this Mediterranean restaurant, across the street and a block away north. If they both remembered their dreams, they could discuss them over food. That sounded like a date. He liked that she wasn't shy.

When he got home, he had Scotch on the rocks. One after another. He felt as if he had made progress with his problem. Then for 'harmonious balance' as she had said, he sipped on a cup of sleepy herbal tea, he brewed from a tea bag she had dug out of her purse during the meal. He'd buy her a box of herbal teabags for tomorrow's date. Cheaper than flowers and more lasting!

He dimmed the lights in the living room and wondered if he should try to sleep. He hears a scratching noise behind him. He had no pets. The stereo and the TV were off. What was that? He looked behind the couch. Moved it away from the wall. A big vinegaroon was catching a black bug. They were scary looking with their two big pincers held forward like weapons, like a scorpion, but he had learned from one of his ex-girlfriends that they were harmless.

Only ate other bugs. He turned off the living room lights and turned on the one in his bedroom. The crunching sound made him look down. There were dozens of shiny black bugs around his feet. He was glad he hadn't taken off his shoes. He ran to his bed and jumped on it. There were too many bugs for one vinegaroon. He did not know if he had any bug spray in the house. Maybe an old can under the kitchen sink. He'd wait until morning to get it. He tossed his shoes on the floor, aiming for some of the bugs. One of them deployed some wings. It flew straight at him, straight for his chest. A conenose bug. He remembered that in his childhood house, sometimes in the summer, those vampire bugs would come inside. When they bit him, he would get a big welt and his mother would dab the bump with cider vinegar. He tried to swat at the flat bug, but it ignored him and stuck its long nose into his heart and started sucking his blood, swelling up like a tick, getting huge. The sharp pain woke him up.

He turned on the light. No welts. No bugs. No pain. Just sleepy and feeling like throwing up. He was getting really tired of these stupid dreams.

~~~

He met her at the Mediterranean restaurant. It smelled good inside. They ordered dishes to share and chose a table near the window. "I always need to see outside, when in an enclosed space," she explained. She was dressed in a grey and white striped skirt suit, with a silky pink shirt under the jacket. She had good-looking legs over simple, black, low pumps. Must be her official work suit. No makeup, just a soft pink lipstick. He liked that she had dressed up for him. He had made an effort too. Wore his blue shirt that, he had been told, showed off his brown eyes. His tight black pants showed off his hot butt. His Italian loafers were freshly shined.

They ate, drank and laughed a lot. Over some honeyed, pistachio pastry, she got to the dreams. She recounted hers first.

She had just entered this large courtroom with her firm's top dog. As soon as they walked in, her boss had pushed her to the bench and told her she was in charge. He would sit right behind her. She had worked on the case, knew all the details, including the fact that the client was guilty. It was a criminal case. A rich brat who had raped and killed his girlfriend, and thought he could get away with it. Before at his arraignment, he had pleaded not guilty. When her turn came to defend her client, she started stuttering, unable to say a single intelligible sentence. She could not stop stammering, the whole courtroom staring, laughing at her. Then at once, she had screamed at the top of her lungs, her words finally coherent: "Guilty, guilty, guilty, Your Honor!" to the judge and the whole courtroom. And that had woken her up.

She had experienced that dream a few times

before, always a little different, but basically the same. She explained that talking in public was her fear, her fear of not being adequate, of forgetting her arguments, of being unable to defend the clients she knew were lying, of being less than what her firm expected of her.

He recounted his first dream, five days before, of being caught in a flood, the water chasing and catching up to him. He skipped the few dreams he thought too personal, too revealing maybe, about his fears of not being sexually adequate, about his fear of dying. Then went on to the previous night's dream. About the bugs, and the vinegaroon unable to eat them all, and the one disgusting vampire bug, sucking the life out of his heart.

She interpreted the first one, as being overwhelmed by something important to him at that time, something he had not dealt with well, something that may drown him if he did not deal with the problem. This other dream probably meant that something was still "bugging" him. Dreams spoke in metaphors. Someone or something was sucking him dry, probably someone close to him. She said that he should look at what event or events recently happened to trigger these nightmares.

Feeling uncomfortable about sharing his worries and needing some time to reflect upon what he had just learned, he changed the subject. "How did they come up with the word nightmares? Female horses in the dark, triggering unspoken fears?" She replied:

"You're not too far! People rode horses before cars, and the dark ones invaded their subconscious mind." They agreed to skip meeting during the week-end and reconnect after work, next Monday.

~~~

Looking out the window, he could see a tall woman in a flowing dark green shift walking in the middle of his street, coming toward his house. It was surprising that there were no cars on the road that evening. The woman almost seemed to be floating, her long dark hair streaming behind her angular face. She moved to the sidewalk as a delivery truck drove by. He went outside and walked to her, attracted by her demeanor. When he got close to her, he felt her piercing yellow-green eyes search his face. Did she need a ride? She slowed down and stopped, as if daring him to come closer. Had he met her before? He could not remember. As he was closing in, he felt compelled and repulsed at the same time. A few feet from her, he stopped and looked at her. He wanted to ask her who she was. What did she want? Where she was going? But the words would not come out. He thought he had met her before. He was fascinated by her mesmerizing eyes. Although the street was still, quiet and damp, there must have been a slight wind that rippled her hair. Her dress swept back and he noticed her bare feet. Dark green, scaly, clawed. As she raised her hands toward his face, he saw that these were also green claws. He did not understand. When she opened her mouth, showing sharp, pointed teeth, he screamed long and hard, unable to stop.

Once again the sheets were drenched in sweat. Again, it was three in the morning. He did not know if he should get up or go back to sleep. He was so shaken up, he knew he could not lay down again. He showered, trying to rinse away all the fears he had just experienced.

Did he walk outside earlier? Did he dream or hallucinate the green she-monster? This was not the sweet pink and grey woman he had dined with earlier. Who was that creature? Growing up, he thought his mother was a reptile, mean and cold. Was that a dream about his mother? He had felt relief and then guilt, when she had passed away a few years back. Was that her ghost?

He devoured a big breakfast, then called his old school buddy back east. Six o'clock there, he should be awake.

"Long time, man! What have you been up to?" They talked about their respective jobs, their common lack of family, their respective hobbies, both binge drinking and binge watching serial thrillers, watching football games they only cared about because their co-workers cared about them, and also going for quick, unsatisfying, passionless relationships.

"So what's up, man. What's going on?" He recounted some of his dreams, feeling a little guilty about laying it all on him at once. "You've been watching too many cheap sci-fi movies. I gotta be at work in one hour, cover for my boss. But all I have to say is: you need to find you a good woman. That will cure you!" The buddy said as he hung up.

~~~

He thought about the accident that had happened on the day of his mother's funeral. He had gotten there two hours late. Everyone in the parlor seemed to be furious at him. He was certain everyone could smell the booze on him. She had hated anyone drinking alcohol, her husband having done his share of drinking throughout his life. So there was not going to be a wake. Besides, a wake was for talking about the good things the dead ones had done during their life. He could not think of anything that merited a wake for his mother.

He had always bought and brought flowers to her grave. After apologizing for not always being a good kid, for not becoming a lawyer, as she had wanted, he would leave feeling empty and insecure. He remembered at once that this day was the anniversary of her passing away. What that what this was all about? She had raised him, fed and housed him, supported him until it was time to go to college. She had never been a loving person, but she had always been there for him, even when his dad had been hurt and had left their home, ashamed of his injuries.

He called the sweet hippy girl. "I could use you

this evening. It's the fourth anniversary of my mother's dying of brain cancer. I'm having a hard time with it. Can you come over?"

That night, he did not remember his dreams, but slept all night, with a new warm body, right next to him.

~~~

Four Wings

4

She was soaring high, spiraling into a warm ascending current. She had to find rodents for her two fledglings. They were so hungry all the time. Not quite ready to fly out of the nest, but she hoped it would happen soon. She was spending so much effort looking for food for them, she hardly had time to enjoy flying or to stop to eat a good meal.

Way below, the land was shimmering from the heat, making it hard for her to see the small details on the ground. She spotted two ravens, sitting on top of a tall, barren tree. Her acute hearing listened to them as they rapidly stammered something about dangerous food. A small poisonous snake at the foot of their dried-up tree. They could have it. It would not be enough for her two youths.

She rode up higher, moving to the East, away from the sun, to steeper hills. After she passed over the top of a sharp ridge, the currents swirled her downward. With her keen eyes, she spotted a fat packrat on the shady side of a mesquite shrub. She was still a few hundred wing spans above it, but she needed to plan her attack. Earlier, she had spotted its large nest near the base of a piñon, an unmistakable mound of juniper branches, dried cow manure, cholla fruits, grasses, and feathers. If it sensed her attack, the smart rodent would make a beeline for its nest, from the small-leaved bush it was gathering beans at.

The hawk took her time. There were a few bunches of tall grasses between the shrub and the packrat's nest. She kept on slowly circling downward, refraining from flapping her wings, and careful to keep her shadow away from the fat rodent. It had started carrying its bounty up the hill. Most likely a female, with babies inside, it stopped on the side of a clump of grass. This was the moment the red tail chose to attack. She folded her wings and dove faster than the fiercest wind. She landed, claws extended, right on top of the packrat. Her weight broke the furry critter's back. While still on the ground, she cut off and ate the head. Then she picked up the limp body in one of her claws and lifted herself in the air.

When she arrived at her nest, perched high on top of a Ponderosa pine, her daughter was pecking the head of the male. She was the dominant one, born first, a little bigger, a little stronger than her brother, and almost ready to take her first flight. Both fledglings threw themselves at the fresh kill. They ripped the rodent apart and finished it in a short time. Still hungry, the young female kept pecking at her mother's beak. This was not enough food. She would have to bring them back more, and soon.

This time, she winged towards the humans' hay barn. This could be dangerous to fly over, but it was usually an easy place to find prey with water, hay and grain close together, unless the dogs were running around. The cats were no problems, more scared of her than of the dogs. Everything was quiet. The dogs were sleeping on the other side of the compound, in the shade of the smelly vehicles. She spotted a juvenile rabbit and dove on it. Another perfect kill. They never saw her coming when she came down so fast from high above them.

But the rooster in the hen house, had seen her too. He was sounding the alarm. The dogs ran to the chicken coop, barking loudly. She was already up in the air, and flying as fast as she could with the heavy cottontail in her grip. She did not notice the human coming out of his house.

She felt the pain before she heard the shot. Her right wing was burning. Excruciating. Useless. She could not fly. As she was falling, she hoped her young ones were old enough to soar from their nest. Still holding on to the rabbit, she crashed to the ground, breaking her neck on impact.

~~~

3

This new body was hot and wet. A perfect space. The soul had wanted a warm place, a friendly family to live with, and a way to work outside all day long.

    He was born inside the round mud house on a sunny day. After he was cleaned, the midwife took him outside, in the sunshine, to meet his father. "Your first born is a boy", she exclaimed. The man tenderly took the baby into his arms. "This is good! I will call you Mosi. I have long waited for someone to work the land and tend the goats with me".

    Mosi followed and helped his father as best he could. It was hard keeping up with this tall man's long strides. Later he spent four days in school, every week for four years. The first year, his mother walked with him for the two kilometers there, his older sister in tow, his younger one strapped to her back. Often time during that year, his father would pick him up after school. They would take different paths, according to how hot the sun was that day. On the way home or to the pastures, his father would teach him about the different animals, the edible and the poisonous plants, and where the good roots and mushrooms hid. Mosi thought it was more useful to know about the land, than what he was learning at school.

    After that first year, he had to walk to the schoolhouse by himself. He became strong and fearless.

When he got home, there was farm work and goat tending. His mother took care of the milking every morning, and they had fresh milk and fruits for breakfast. He learned to butcher goats, and chickens, and wild game, and of ways to preserve the meat. He raised a frail chick from one of the hens. This little bird he named Kuku, grew to full size and would follow him around the house and the yard, but knew to stay home when Mosi was moving the goats. The boy learned to respect all beings, from people, to animals and plants.

One day, he overheard his father talk about war amongst the local tribes. A war about spiritual beliefs, he had said. Even neighbors killing neighbors. His father told him there would not be anymore schooling for a while, until peace came back to the village.

The days were getting a little shorter. The rains had not been generous that year. Mosi and his father took the goats up the mountain to find better forage. The land was drying up. They had to bring the livestock back to the valley for water every night. As they climbed up the hill, the buck became very nervous. He kept circling the herd, guarding them from straying too far, bringing back right away the two young does who would always venture from the others.

His father was walking ahead, when at once he turned around and told Mosi to stop pushing the goats, to hide in the thicket, and wait for him. The tall man lowered himself, and then almost on all fours, he crept up to the top of the ridge.

After looking at the other side for a little while, his father came running back to him, scattering the goats down hill in the process. "Run Mosi, run and tell your mother and your sisters to go hide in the small cave next to the spring. You hide there too, and I will find you after I take the goats back." "But Father?" exclaimed Mosi. "No, run! Now! Go!"

He ran. He ran so fast he did not even notice hanging from a branch, the green snake that could have bit him. When he got to the house, short of breath, he told his mother what his father had said. She pushed him and his sisters out the door with a package of dried food she had prepared a while before. "Run! Don't stop until you get to the little cave. Make sure there are no animals inside before you go in. Father and I will find you later. I'm going to wait for him. Go! Go!"

Mosi grabbed Kuku under his arm, then he and his sisters ran to the cave. At the spring, he filled a couple of skins with the clear, cold water. He checked the cave, but it was dry and empty. He gathered some big leaves to sit on and covered the entrance with branches. They waited. They ate and finally fell asleep as the night came on.

In the morning, neither their mother or father had shown up at the cave. Mosi was very worried. His younger sister was crying softly and clinging to her sister. She was also clutching Kuku, so hard that she almost choked him. Mosi wanted to run to the house, his older sister told him to wait a little longer.

The next day, Mosi left early while his sisters were still sleeping. He ran, hiding behind trees to stop and breathe, before running again. When he got close to the hut, he felt bile rising up to his mouth. There was an aura of fear and a smell of decay all around him. He slowed down, crouched, stopped and stared at the carnage. The goats had been slaughtered. The meat left to rot and be eaten by hyenas and vultures. Not one chicken in sight.

No sounds came from the jungle, as when a large predator prowled nearby. Mosi wanted to call out his parents, but every fiber in him shouted danger. Slowly, quietly, he crept to the hut. The door was slightly ajar. He could hear the flies buzzing before he got in.

Behind the door, his father's whole body was soaked in blood and flies, his head separated, off to one side. On their bed, his mother was naked, the inside of her legs and her birth pouch caked with dried blood, her throat partly slashed open. With a rasping voice, as red foam slowly bubbled out of her mouth with every word, she said: "Go to your aunt Sadiki! From the spring, go down the stream, then to the big river, past the first village, then cross the river to the next village. Her hut has two tall spears in front of the door. I will not be alive for much longer. Do not come back here. You are the head of the family now. Take care of your sisters." She stopped and her eyes rolled inside her head, fear showing on her face. Her breath was shallow and slowing down.

He lingered until she passed, a few minutes later. He covered her damaged body with a bedding cloth. He knew that she had waited for him, despite the pain she was suffering.

His father's machete was gone, but he found the big kitchen knife his mother kept under the sink. He left and closed the door. Outside, the danger was still suffocating him with every breath he took. He went to look at the scattered remains of goats, mostly horned heads and hip bones. He counted them twice. Eight, only eight. Maybe, one got away. Maybe, the murdering rebels took one with them. Reluctantly, he slipped back into the jungle, knowing he needed to let the hyenas and the vultures finish cleaning up.

He felt drawn to the shade of a large tree. Cautiously, he looked all around, and found a trail of ants moving toward a thick undergrowth. There he found the last goat. One of her front leg was broken, bent forward at an odd angle, the hoof touching her nose. She was not stiff yet. She must have just died. With his mother's very sharp knife, he cut both hind quarters and back-straps. He wrapped the meat in large leaves, while fighting flying and crawling insects. Then, moving from shade to shade, he went back to the little spring's cave.

Although his instinct told him to get away from their home as soon as possible, Mosi waited for his sisters to digest the news that their parents were never coming back. A couple of days later, loaded with dried meat and water, they traveled early in the morning and late in the evening when there was just enough light to see danger, and to find shelter for the night. After three days, they reached the first village. People looked suspiciously at them, at first. Then, an older woman waved for them to come into her house. She fed them, asked them if they wanted to give her Kuku. Mosi told her that he was the only chicken he had left, and how his family and all their animals had been killed by the rebels. Many of the villagers were gathered outside, listening in on either side of the curtained door. When Mosi finished telling the woman about their misfortunes, the people outside had many questions. They wanted to know who were the rebels, where they were going next, what their tribe's name was. But Mosi did not know. He had just run away with his sisters, and was going to see his aunt further down river.

When everyone outside had quieted down and left, the old woman asked the children to spend the night and to be on their way the next day. They agreed, ate a warm meal, and slept well for the first time since they had left their home.

They followed the river, crossing once where it was wide and shallow. They found a well-travelled trail a few paces from the water's edge. It felt safe. They were still worried about being seen, but now they travelled longer distances in daylight, occasionally meeting someone going the other way. Two days later, they reached their aunt's village.

Sadiki was older than their mother. She had lost

her husband, and her children had gone to a bigger settlement, for better wages, for easier living. She welcomed the children, told them they could stay as long as they wanted. Mosi helped with the animals, the girls with the gardens.

A few months later, Sadiki let them know about rumors of terrorists roaming the countryside, raping and killing people for no apparent reason. She was worried for their safety. Their aunt told them about the town where her oldest daughter lived. All three would be able to stay with her, go to school, and later earn money and raise a family where it would be safe.

Mosi took his sisters to his cousins' in the big town three days away. It was going to be an easy life for the girls, but not for him. It was a foreign world. He felt he was too old for school now. He was growing hair below his belly. Soon, he would be a man.

He travelled upstream, making one stop with Sadiki, to let her know how her daughter was doing, how his sisters liked living in a town. Then he left to see his birthplace again, despite his mother's warnings about coming back.

He thought the bugs would have cleaned up the flesh from the bones, and he could take the bones outside and cover them with stones. After the house was cleaned up, he would set fire to it, and build himself a small hut closer to the river, but not near a village. He would live just by himself, raise a few chickens, fish like Aunt Sadiki had taught him, and have a small garden. It would be a nice simple life, without inconveniencing anyone, without anyone bothering him.

As he got close to his family's home, he relived seeing his parents' mutilations. He was so sad, he did not sense the danger behind him until the last moment. As he turned around to face it, he raised his right arm to fend it off. The sharp machete sliced off the flesh from his forearm and shattered his bone. He did not know the man attacking him, but he recognized his father's machete.

He ran into the jungle, holding his broken arm to his chest. He hid during the night between two damp, rotten logs. He slept fitfully until light began to point between the tall canopies above. After brushing the bugs off his wound, he made his way to the little spring's cave.

He was hot. He could not feel his arm. The fever was already clouding his mind. His dreams were filled with attacking wild men and beasts. In the morning, the sky was ablaze. A radiant white. He saw his mother and his father opening their arms, and inviting him into their new hut. He willingly rejoined them.

~~~

2

It had been Syvne's mistake. She was always making mistakes. Her first mistake was to be born in the middle of the long cold, during a great shake that split the frozen ground of the tundra. Maybe she should not have been born at all. The flap to the chum had opened while her mother was giving birth. The whole reindeer-hide tipi had shook on its own when she was born, letting snow blow in. Her mother had put her to her breast, and covered her with her furs, leaving herself half-naked. Then she bled and froze during the night. That was what her father had said, many times, whenever she would ask for her mother. When she was born, Syvne brought a curse on the whole tribe.

As soon as she could walk some distance, she was relegated to the back of the sledge trains. She was not worth the value of one of the tribe's black and white dogs. At times, when she was lagging too far behind, the older wrinkled woman driving the last sledge, would pick up the small child and toss her on top of the coaster, where she would quickly fall asleep. When the reindeer train would stop, she would be pushed roughly to the side, so the men would not be angered by the old one's kind gesture.

When Syvne got her first blood, she had to stay behind, away from the herd, so as not to cause any more harm than what she had already done. As the white sun cleared the horizon, she could no longer see the last reindeer, she slipped into her sleep bag: two deer hides stitched together, with the hair inside, the only thing left from her Mother.

    She slept for a while, until a crackling sound woke her up with a start. Green lights were arching into the night. She watched them as they changed shapes. After a while, a swirling rope appeared, seeming to come out of the ground and shooting to the stars. A pink glow below, turning into a green light above. If he had been there, her father would have told her that she had conjured the darkness below her and she would never be able to climb to the sky. He was sure Syvne had been ensorcelled at birth, by the evil twin below the ground, and that would certainly bring despair and death to the tribe. This was why she had to stay behind the reindeer, to bring back any strays, to be the last one to close the train.

    As she kept looking at the shimmering light, it changed into a huge eagle, green with yellow highlights. She liked watching the golden and brown eagles soar above in the daytime, she had always dreamed of training a young one for company. This night's giant eagle, made of bright green, vertical rays, separated from the frozen ground, spread its wings and rose above the snow. She knew this vision was just for her. This beautiful sight must have been sent by her mother's spirit. Syvne thought that the tribe would not miss her. Her father would not miss her. The only one who may miss her, was the elder woman on the last sledge. Old Grandmother had even tossed her a reindeer's frozen shoulder before they left her behind. In three days, they would be far away. Even if she ran, it would be hard to catch up with them.

The green light shaped like an eagle was a sign to soar on her own, to look for her destiny, or to seek her final days. She got out of her sleep bag, placed the frozen meat inside, as well as some dry moss, and rolled the whole thing up. She tied the bundle with reindeer sinew and slung it across her back. It was still night, but the aurora lit up her path. Slowly, she started walking north, toward the long cold that was calling her, waiting for her. She hoped that in the frozen forest above, a giant bear was waiting for her too.

~~~

1

When Habib first saw her, he was certain she was a djinn or the daughter of Tanith, the mother goddess of rain. Light, auburn locks poked out of a blue lace scarf framing her pearly skin and rosy cheeks, while her clear-blue eyes stared intently at him. The beautiful child was softly rounded, her already shapely figure revealed under the lavender, high-waisted dress that all the rich elite wore these days. On either side, she was flanked by her ladies-in-waiting. One, a sturdy Italian matron, was examining Habib sternly, her arms folded across her chest, the other, a pretty, veiled woman, looking down at the tiled floor, was holding one of her hands, like a friend. Malek, the older gentleman who had entered with the three women, introduced the enchanting child as Amira, his future bride, and the young, veiled woman as Latifa, his latest wife.

Habib's father, Mossadak, invited them to sit down in the open-aired living room, which offered a splendid view of the Atlas Mountains on this bright day. Then, he turned to his son and asked him to have his mother bring mint tea, dates and pistachio pastries.

After exchanging news about the weather, the state of the land, the current politics, Malek came to the point of his visit. "I will marry Amira when she comes of chid-bearing age. For our wedding, I want you to create the most exquisite bed, a bed that will reflect her beauty and my love for her. I will pay you generously, in silver, as usual. You have one year to fashion this treasure for my lovely Amira."

Both young women looked down at the floor, while the Italian matron gazed in the distance outside the latticed windows. Mossadak agreed, telling Malek that he had just finished curing long, thick planks of cedar that would be perfect for such a piece. The two elder men left to look at the wood in the shop.

While they were gone, Habib showed the three women the brown kestrel he had rescued a few years before. Once out of his large cage, the handsome bird perched on his gloved left hand. Amira came close to see it, so close that the boy could smell her delicate perfume. Her plump lips were almost at his fingers' reach. His head was spinning. He was getting lost in the depth of her light blue eyes. The small falcon clacked his short beak and Amira quickly stepped back, breaking the spell, just before the two older men returned to the room.

Mossadak was the most renowned artist-woodworker in all of the country. He used local wood, mostly cedar and olive wood, dried carefully, inspected for quality and insect holes, then he stored the prepared timber in his warehouse. People sometimes, would wait years for him to make them a piece of furniture.

Mossadak asked his son to design the bed for

Malek and Amira. While never neglecting his formal studies of math, religion, political science, and three foreign languages, Habib apprenticed under his father from the time he could hold a chisel and a mallet. As Mossadak aged, arthritis developed in his hands and his eyes were starting to fail him. Soon after, his five mentees and Habib were building furniture and smaller objects, from start to finish, under the old master's watchful eyes.

A week passed before Malek returned, this time accompanied by a tall dark valet, but without the women. Habib was studying in a corner of the large living-room with his French tutor. He was disappointed that Amira had not shown.

Mossadak showed the silver merchant the drawings of the bed. Carved on the center of the headboard, two swans were intertwined, their long necks coiled. Feather cutouts decorated either sides of the panel. The four sturdy feet of the bed were decorated with a lighter-colored wood inlays of small swans. Malek was impressed by the design. He asked that the headboard be solid all the way, but with ivory inlays of feathers where the cutouts would have been, in the bas-relief of the two swans, their eyes should be inlayed with ivory, and the small swans on the legs should also be carved of ivory. He had some thin slices of elephant ivory on hand and would send them to the shop. The older men agreed on a price. The servant paid the full amount in silver. Before he left, Malek asked whether Amira would be able to study Arabic and French with Habib until their wedding, as he did not want her to be in school with the common people. After one quick look at his son, Mossadak agreed.

Twice a week Amira came to their house for language tutoring, under the watchful eyes of the Italian matron. Habib was in love with the young girl, but knew better than to show any affection toward her. His father had told him about Malek's four wives and how he was supposed to behave with Amira.

Mossadak had known Malek for a long time and rarely agreed with his older friend, especially on the scriptures of the Koran. They would often talk politics, although they both had very different opinions. Malek believed only those in power should rule the country, they should be of the upper class, educated and rich, and that poor people were of a lesser class, much like animals. Habib's father believed that all persons were equal, regardless of race, gender, education, or financial worth, and that honest and honorable people from each class should have a say-so in governing. Although both men followed the same faith, Mossadak also thought that one wife was enough for one man. Their divergent political opinions held in his study, would often lead to heated conversations that seeped right through the wooden doors of the old clay brick building.

During the lessons, at times the plump Italian companion would excuse herself for a few minutes, to visit the kitchen and sample Habib's mother's delicious pastries. At first, during these short interludes, the two adolescents would only exchange short glances. A few weeks later they were gazing longer at each other and would smile, careful not to utter a word, as they both knew any verbal contact would not be permissible. When Amira started becoming proficient in French, they tried to play word games in that language, but the tutor let them know that they were to remain formal when addressing each other.

After Amira and her chaperone left, Habib would go to work in the wood shop, eager to continue the carving of the swans, while dreading the day when his unrequited love would no longer be able to participate in his studies, when it would be time for her to marry the older man.

Amira was a fast learner. Both children knew the French teacher came from north of the sea, from France, where people were more lenient than the Italian matron. One day the lesson was about parents and ancestors. Amira shared with Habib that her father had died after a horse accident, and that her mother had been obliged to go live with her uncle. The uncle inherited all of her parents possessions and he was the one who had solicited Malek for her marriage.

All at once, Habib touched Amira's hand to comfort her, the kestrel clacked his beak, and the Italian governess returned from the kitchen. Although the boy had quickly removed his hand, the matron had spotted the gesture. She dug out a dark scarf from her pocket and covered Amira's face with it. Then she grabbed the girl's hand and pulled her roughly out of the house, telling the teacher that there would be no more French or Arabic lessons for her.

A month later, Mossadak sent Malek a message that the bed was finished and could be picked up. With the same courier, Malek replied that he wanted Habib to deliver the bed. With the two strongest woodworkers carrying the sturdy bed, Habib took the lead, singing all the way, dreaming of seeing Amira again.

Malek shook the solid frame, admired the two carved swans, then checked the ivory inlays. Satisfied, he told two of his servants to bring the bed inside his palace and put it in the blue room. He sent the two woodworkers home and turned to Habib: "Do impart to your father that he has carved a beautiful piece of furniture, as I expected. And now, I want to show you a beautiful animal I own. Follow me."

Habib suddenly had a nagging feeling that the old man was not as pleased as he said. Not a single woman could be seen anywhere. He followed Malek to the stables. As they were walking, the richly dressed man was talking. "You have studied the scriptures, yes." Not giving him time to answer, he continued: "Before our current government, do you know what happened to a man who steals from another man?"

They had arrived at the stables. Habib did not

fully understanding what was implied, but suddenly felt the urge to run. On Malek's signal, two coarse-looking flunkies came out, grabbed the boy's ams and dragged him inside the barn. The smell of hay, horse sweat, and hot manure overpowered his senses. Something was terribly wrong. The men forced him to kneel by a stump, still holding both arms. Malek continued: "A thief must have his right hand cut off so that he can no longer steal, so everyone will know of his crime! You have stolen the heart of my Amira. You are a thief!" A third man came out of a stall where a stunning, black Arabian horse was prancing nervously. The man was wielding a large, ornate sword. Habib's arm was placed on the stump and with a broad circling motion of the sword, his right hand was cut off. The boy screamed, as blood spurted out of his forearm. Kicking his stall door open, the magnificent stallion ran out of the barn, brushing past the impassive Malek, with a mournful whine.

Habib's mother bandaged his arm, which he held over his chest. After he told his father what had happened, Mossadak removed the falcon from his cage and threw him outside into the air. The bird screeched once as he flew toward the full moon sitting on the horizon. Mossadak told the crying Habib: "You have dishonored our family, you, my only son. From this day on, you will study the scriptures in the back of the shop and never be seen in public again."

That night, Habib dreamed he lived where no

one else would, that he could fly with his bird to far away lands, and never return.

~~~

One Lonely Beach

"No, Mama, I'm a boy!" The two-year old girl told her mother. The psychologist thought it best to leave the child in her fantasy. It would pass.

But it did not. The following year, she wanted her name changed to Jean Michel. "Why a French name? Mikaela is a beautiful name your father and I chose very carefully."

"It's not even a boy's name! My real name is Jean Michel."

Now and then, her parents would humor her by calling her by the French name.

In kindergarten, her understanding teacher would use the boy's name that she had insisted upon the very first day. She played so well with the other children when her wishes were observed. Even her parents were swayed over and started using masculine pronouns when talking to the child. While at work, her mother took time out to study gender orientation and split personalities.

When Jean Michel started elementary school, he asked for French language classes and geography.

Since it was not available at the school, his father took it upon himself to teach him the geography of France and the few rudimentary phrases he remembered from university. Jean Michel was soon excelling in school and at the evening lessons offered by his father.

They got him an audio set to continue learning French. He listened to it for an hour each day after school. A couple of months later, while bicycling with his mother in a big park in Copenhagen, a few blocks from their home, he met Martin, a young boy of French descent. Although Martin was two years older than Jean Michel, they became friends immediately. The younger child's gender was never questioned.

Martin was interested in the history of France. He mentioned how his great-grandmother was born and lived in Dunquerque, on the coast of northern France, until she moved to Denmark before the nazi invasion.

Jean Michel was very absorbed by an area not too far from there, called Dieppe. Martin had asked him if he had been there. "Oh, it was a long time ago. During the war," had casually replied Jean Michel. His mother had heard the comment and wondered when her son had been introduced to war. They never exposed him to violent shows, or even to competitive games. Through the school or the library, perhaps? She worried that she had cocooned him too long. Mikaela had seemed so fragile when she was born. The stories told were only from children's books, with the wicked witch almost winning, but the good always prevailing at the end.

The two boys went on to play toy soldiers games in Jean's room. On the walls, the boy had all the cute, fantastic, pastel-colored animals removed and replaced with images and drawings of small boats and long quiet beaches. Both parents had accepted his desires, and now fully supported his concept of living in an alternate gender.

One of his favorite classes, was art. He would spend the whole hour on his own projects rather than follow the teacher's lead. When clay was brought into the class one day, Jean Michel made a huge angular structure, although he was told to make a small object so that everyone's class assignments could fit in the kiln. A picture of the massive rectangular building was taken for him to bring home. Jean Michel, angered that the size of his sculpture was not acceptable, destroyed it with quick chops of his hand, while the clay was still soft.

When Jean showed the picture of the clay building to Martin, the older boy told him it looked like the blockhaus pictures his father had shown him. Rectangular, with just one square entrance, no windows, but for a few slits just below the roofline. Before he was born, Martin's father had lost his grandmother and went to her birthplace near Dunquerque to spread her ashes. He had taken pictures of the beach and one of the German fortresses looked just like that. Martin said he would borrow the pictures from his father to show him.

When Jean Michel saw the picture of the blockhaus on the beach near Dunquerque, he said that was exactly what he had built, with only a few small disparities. The two of them opened Jean's father's computer to look at beaches in Dieppe. They found a blockhaus that had partly sunk into the sand and was sitting lopsided in front of steep cliffs. It looked ominous on that deserted beach.

For the next few days, Jean Michel kept asking his parents for the strangest things:

- "We have to go to Dieppe right away!"
- "I need to see my sister's child." Yet, Jean Michel did not have any siblings.
- "I live at the secret house." When asked about this mysterious place, all he would tell them was that everybody nearby knew about the secret. It was even written on a wall.
- "I need to remove my body." That last sentence was one that alarmed his parents the most. They were afraid he was loosing his sanity, that he may commit suicide even at that early age. His father remembered an ad for a medium: 'Looking for answers in difficult times, just ask Lady Esmeralda.' It showed a wizened-faced woman in front of a crystal ball. At first, his mother had declared the whole thing utter nonsense, that they could no longer support his lunacy. Finally, when Jean Michel asked to go find his body, so he could be properly buried, his mother relented. "Let's go see the medium."

A week later, in the suburb of the capital, on the south side of the main canal, the boy and both parents arrived at the medium's place. It was a shabby little house, painted bright yellow with turquoise trims, in the middle of a small unkempt yard but for a couple of large white geraniums on either side of the front door. The older woman welcomed them inside and immediately asked to be paid in advance. "Sometimes, people don't like what I tell them, I do not lie or paint them only a rosy picture, but if it doesn't fit what they want to hear, then they want to leave without paying." They paid her.

"It's for the child, isn't it." Jean Michel's father nodded. The medium lit a small chunk of myrrh, then blew over the coal. Its earthy smell invaded the cramped room. She gazed into a large, clear, faceted crystal while fingering small rosary beads. The room was suddenly very cold. She shivered as if a chill had run down her spine. She closed her eyes, and the boy seemed very distressed. He started crying. In French, he whispered: *"Mais non, je n'ai rien fait!"* [No, I didn't do anything!]

The old seer told them that they must listen to the boy. He had come back in this lifetime to deal with what was left undone in another life. She told them to act soon, as the boy was starting to drift into another dimension and could become lost in it.

On the way home, Jean's parents decided that the old woman could be right. It was time to find out what was going on with their child. They decided to leave the following week for Dieppe, on the coast of France. They made reservations for a few days at a Bed-and-Breakfast not far from the beach, and a train trip from Copenhagen to Rouen. From there they would rent a car.

Jean Michel was elated, talking in French the whole time. He would spend hours studying the second world war in France. His parents did not share his enthusiasm, but went along with his research. Their ancestors had suffered much in Denmark during that war.

A week later, when they got to Dieppe in the middle of the day, it was damp and windy. The tide was high. The smell of the ocean permeated the air. They walked around the small town. At one point Jean Michel pointed out to a two-storied building. "That's where I lived." Letters engraved on the corner house wall read: 'Rue du Secret'. The boy wanted to go inside the house and meet its inhabitants. They knocked on the old wooden door, but there was no answer. Partially broken-down shutters covered every window. The home felt empty. An old man passing by told them that no one lived there but ghosts. He made the sign of the cross as he left hurriedly.

The next morning, they went to the beach early, while the tide was low. The beach was deserted. In the distance, a few fishing boats danced on the ocean. The boy stared at them longingly. Just below the cliffs, like a beached whale, a massive building with a yawning crack above the square door, had sunk partly into the sand. There were no windows to look inside. A large chain and padlock on the thick wooden door forbade any entrance into the building. Jean Michel was both frightened and disappointed. His father told him he would go talk to the mayor the next day to find out if they could get in.

The following day, the sun was shining, making the small town look more inviting. The mayor set up an appointment with the gate-keeper of the blockhaus for the next morning. He also told them about the Devereux family, which had been the last name Jean Michel had used when introducing himself to the portly man.

"Yvette Devereux lost most of her family during the war. Her father, her husband, and her three sons. All the old-timers will tell you that she went mad and died in her house at the corner of the Rue du Secret. My grand-father used to tell me the same thing. That house has remained vacant since then. Her daughter has tried to sell it many times, but anyone interested has heard crying and seen ghosts when they set foot in it. The house is falling apart. The town has thought of making it a historical monument, a museum of sorts, but we have run into problems with funding every time we tried to purchase it."

The mayor provided the address of Jeanette Devereux, the only living descendant in Dieppe, and told them that he would attend the opening of the blockhaus at ten o'clock the next morning.

Jean Michel insisted they go see Mrs. Devereux

right away. By now, his parents were captivated by the whole story unfolding in front of them. They no longer doubted their child; they wanted this mystery resolved. They drove to the small village north of Dieppe and knocked on an old stone house, covered with green and blue lichens. A young woman invited them in and went to get the lady of the house.

The living room was filled with memorabilia. Framed old sepia pictures on the walls, on the old wooden furniture: crocheted cloths on the back of padded chairs, religious porcelain statues, smoking pipes on stands, a few miniature replicas of sailing ships on the counters. All seemed from a distant past. The wind picked up from the open window. The view of the Atlantic seemed to stretch forever to the West. An older lady made her way into the room, clutching a wheeled walker. She stared at Jean Michel, as the young woman helped her to a padded rocking chair.

"Come close, child!" She beckoned in French to the boy. "You look like my aunt's youngest child." She hesitated, then slowly added: "But all the men of her family were swallowed by the war. My aunt never had children again. What's your name, child?" She had spoken to him in French and he answered in the same language. *"Je m'appelle Jean Michel, Madame."* Mrs. Devereux leaned back in the rocking chair with her eyes closed. A couple of tears could be seen out of her sunken eyes.

The Danes watched her for a couple of minutes, afraid of breaking the spell. She finally opened her eyes. *"Pourquoi es tu ici, mon enfant?"* [Why are you here, my child?]. "I need to find my body..." He turned to his parents at a loss for words. "For closure" his father translated. The old lady answered: "My mother told me that her nephew Jean Michel went fishing, when he was a boy during the war. All the men in the family were fighting the enemies. Being too young to fight, he was helping my mother's sister gather food. One day, he went fishing and never came back. His boat was found smashed against the rocks, but his body was never found." Jeanette Devereux continued: "I was just a baby then. My mother told me that her sister went crazy shortly after. She tore up her hair, ripped off her clothes and screamed all the time." Jean Michel interrupted in a firm voice. "I know where my body is!"

The next day found them on the beach in front of the blockhaus. Colorful and obscene graffiti adorned the walls. The gate-keeper, the mayor and other curious locals had come for the grand opening. Jean Michel could not stop shaking. His mother was worried: too much, too soon.

The large wooden door creaked as it reluctantly opened, its bottom eaten away by the sea. The mayor handed Jean Michel a flashlight: "This is your play, young man, isn't it?" The boy took the lamp, and followed by his father who had one hand on his shoulder, he stepped into the damp building.

The cement floor at one time, had been supported by long beam covered with a layer of concrete.

Most of the cement had cracked and fallen between the rotten beams. Carefully, Jean Michel went to the far corner of the blockhaus. "That's me! That's me! Right here in the corner." The bare bones of a small hand, with two long bones attached by sinew, had turned orange with time and salt. The rest of the skeleton was hiding under a chunk of cement. When it became obvious the boy had found the remnants of a body, the mayor had everyone get out. He called the police for a crime scene investigation.

The three Danes drove to Mrs. Devereux to let her know about the find. She agreed to provide a DNA sample to confirm the identity of her nephew. She would let the Danes know of the police's results. She told them that her gut already knew, like Jean Michel's, that they would confirm the bones were her aunt's youngest boy.

When the family arrived in Copenhagen, the child insisted in going shopping for clothes, girl clothes. "This was what I needed to do since I was born. I am Michaela now!" She told her mother with a smile. Her mother smiled too, in response.

~~~

The Road Runner

The truck needed an oil change. Even if they could find a place ready to take them in right away, they had not found enough wait time for the three hours needed to get the fluids and the filters changed. Maybe after this load, they would have time to do it, before the next one. Large crates of onions going to Phoenix today. Hopefully tomorrow evening, they were going to pick up a load of alfalfa not too far from the Mexican border, if it was ready. Then, they would deliver it to a big horse farm, just east of Dallas. If they had to wait for the hay, they may get the oil changed in Tucson. If not, they would make an appointment with a garage in Texas.

They called themselves the B n' B Road Show. Blanche and Bruno, mother and son. The sky blue Peterbilt was beautiful. Blanche had named it Azul the day she had bought it. She had fallen in love with its long nose. None of that flat nose cabover with the engine underneath the seat. She had wanted a rig that could cut the wind, carve the road and be easy to work with. The cabin was big enough for two, even if Bruno got much taller like his dad. She thought those long feet meant he would be tall. Probably six feet tall when done growing. Fourteen years old already, going on twenty. She was proud of her son. His beautiful brown skin, his rust colored eyes with gold flecks, and the way he already handled Azul, when she let him drive on quiet roads. A few years back, she had enrolled him in a good home-school program from England. He excelled in all his courses.

Blanche drove mostly at night. The roads were safer. All the better drivers drove at night. Mostly old timers, who also preferred driving without little cars zipping around them. The produce traveled better that way, rather than during the scorching daytime heat of the Southwest. She cared about her load, and many producers hired her for that reason.

Bruno had adjusted well to their nighttime schedule.

"Hey Mom, watch out for that guy. He can't stay in his lane."

"I see him. He must be falling asleep," she answered.

The big truck in front of them was carrying heavy equipment. He would speed up too fast, making his load swing from side to side. Then he'd slow down to straighten out, riding the middle of the road. Blanche made sure to stay far back. She flashed her brights at the heavy rig, but it didn't make any difference. She tried the radio, but no one knew who that was. The guy did not answer. Idaho plates. A northerner!

THE ROAD RUNNER

Falling asleep at the wheel on those long straight roads. By now, there were three more semis behind them. It was going to be a long night if this guy didn't pull over soon. A small pickup started passing the dangerous truck and had to swerve off on the left shoulder so as not to get hit by the oversized trailer. It honked, but that didn't seem to phase the rig.

But all of the sudden, there was the 'Road Runner'. A vintage pink Corvette showing up out of nowhere, passing them quickly on the left. Bruno was very excited.

"What is she going to do?"

As the little sport car got close to the heedless truck, it beamed its lights, very bright lights. Then more lights popped up on the roof of the car, flashing blue and red, like a cop car. There were no responses from the truck. Then the corvette's horn went off, a very loud horn, like a fog horn. The car drove past the truck and moved right in front of it, staying only a dozen yards ahead of it, lights blinking, horn blaring like an ambulance siren. That seemed to do the trick. The truck driver slowed down, regained control of the trailer, and stayed in its lane. The next exit on the interstate was coming up. The Road Runner took it, followed by the big rig. As they passed the truck on the off ramp, Blanche and Bruno noticed that the pink corvette was gone.

A couple of minutes later, Bruno asked: "Mom. Tell me the story of the Road Runner."

"Again?" She honked at the passing trucks who

had waited so long behind her. Bruno, smiling, shook his head in anticipation.

"Please."

"Alright! The first time I saw her was when I started to drive this rig. I had to get used to its size and wasn't very good at it yet. I'd hog the center lane so I'd know where my right rubber was. Just like you do!" She teased.

"Then all at once they had put down new asphalt on the road. No more dotted line. I was tired, I was late for a delivery, no one was coming from the other side, so I just took the middle of the road. Then I looked down through the window, on my left, and this little pink car was passing me on the left, hugging the break down lane, flashing its brights on this small two-lane highway. I almost jerked the wheel. I got so scared of hitting it. I got back to my lane and The Pink, that's what I called her then, stayed right by my side until I was wide awake and traffic was starting to show up on the other side. That's probably what saved my life, and yours too. I was carrying you then."

Grinning, Bruno said: "Yes, eight months inside you. I wanted to come out. And what did you find out?"

"Okay, wise guy! Two weeks premature wise guy! So I asked on the radio if anyone had seen the Pink. But they hadn't. At the truck stop, I asked a few of them, but no one wanted to talk to this big, pregnant, black woman trucker. Finally, this old guy told me in a hushed voice: 'You're one of the lucky ones, if you saw her. She only shows up if you're in trouble, and if she likes you. Then she helps you if you pay attention. You see, she was in a car wreck on Highway 66, that old road south of I-40. Her and the driver of this short truck had a head on collision. Both were dead on impact. Some cop said it was her fault. She was just a spoiled brat, going too fast in her new car. But I think that she was a good person and that's why she came back. You see, she's making up for killing that driver. That's why the Road Runner helps us truckers.' And as you already know, that's all he told me."

Bruno wasn't satisfied yet.

"Tell me about that other time. What Mateo, that Indian guy, said to you." Blanche sighed as she slowed down. There was a big animal laying down in the right lane. An elk doe. She came to a full stop, a few feet from the big deer. The animal was thrashing around. It seemed unable to stand up. Bruno jumped out of the cab, before his mother could stop him.

"Be careful. She's big. She doesn't know you're trying to help. She might kick you." But he was already running to the elk.

As he reached her and put his hand on her neck, her hooves were thrashing the air, close to Bruno's head. Blanche was worried for her son, but didn't dare get out for fear of aggravating the situation. All of the sudden, an old pink corvette materialized in front of the boy. A white translucent figure with long white hair, got out of the car and approached the animal. Bruno did a double take.

"You're the Road Runner. You're a ghost?"

The woman did not answer, but put her hand on the neck of the big deer, next to the boy's. The elk immediately calmed down. As it tried to get up, Bruno backed up. Hesitant at first, the beast took a few steps towards the barbed wire fence, a few yards away. It shook its head, looked at the boy, then gracefully jumped over the fence and disappeared into the bushes. Bruno turned to thank the white lady, but there was nothing in front of their rig, just empty asphalt and a few elk droppings.

"I saw her. She helped me. Did you see her, Mom?"

Blanche had only seen her son putting his hand on the elk's neck.

"You healed her. I watched her jump the fence."

"Mom, I mean the Road Runner. That's who helped me. She was right there. She did it. She healed the elk. Didn't you see her?" Blanche shook her head.

"I did not. If it was her, she was there for you. I did not need her myself. Maybe the elk was hit by a truck and she felt responsible for the accident. You must be special to have seen her twice in one day. Come on. Let's get moving. We need to deliver these onions."

"Mom, that's what Mateo was telling you. About her being a ghost! He could see her. He saw her when he was driving with you, when he almost had an accident, right?"

"Yes, son. He told me he saw her. She was in the middle of the road. In her white night gown, her long white hair flowing in the wind, that's what he told me. I only saw the car, but I was half asleep. If Mateo hadn't seen her, we would have run into that rig that had flipped over across the highway."

"I feel really special to have seen her. And to have her help me rescue that poor elk. Maybe I can become a veterinarian, or a healer with her help. I'm going to take a nap. Wake me up if you see her again."

Blanche smiled at the innocence of the youth, hoping that she would not need the Road Runner's help any time soon.

~~~

Three Gran Pueblo Lives

This was the fifth time Marika visited Gran Pueblo, a large town with many kivas in an ancient complex of Amerindian ruins, in northern New Mexico. She took pictures each time, as she was fascinated with the whole array. She felt as if she belonged there. It was so familiar. Déjà vu, whenever she went there.

She was in her mid-thirties when she first visited the site, traveling with her young children, camping next to the big pueblo, before there was a visitor center. The third morning there, she left early, having told her children that she would climb on the cliffs above the pueblo to take pictures as the sun rose. She had left them breakfast, in case they woke up before she came back. Their vehicle and their tent were the only ones there. The whole place felt safe.

She had started as a potter a dozen years before, drawing black designs on hand-built clay pots. Early on, she thought she was influenced by the land she lived on. There were many artists using pottery as a medium in New Mexico. A few years later, flipping though artwork books at a university library, she realized many of the designs she drew on her pots resembled those of the Anasazi pottery. All these fine parallel lines, spirals, zigzags and other geometric designs had been drawn on pottery hundreds of years before. Marika studied what little she could find about this mysterious culture. Then she traveled to different old native sites around the Four Corners. Of all the villages she visited, the Gran Pueblo was the one that resonated the most with her.

She could have been a potter there in a past life. She believed that the soul lives eternally; the body is just a temporary shell; and the mind controls the spiritual and the physical bodies during the current lifetime. She also viewed the mind as a trilogy; consisting of the head brain, which directs the conscious and the unconscious; the heart which understands the emotions through empathy; and the stomach which perceives the supernatural, the psychic, the hidden senses.

As Marika took pictures of Gran Pueblo, she knew these were going to be spectacular. The light was just filtering in, intensifying the contrasts of colors, the walls' shadows elongating into the scrubby earth. Smooth light blue over coarse dark brown and beige. She moved her camera just a little with every picture in order to make a collage of the whole site as one. She folded her tripod, put away her camera and descended her perch to rejoin her children.

After they arrived home, she mailed the two rolls of negatives to a company in the Midwest that she had used before with good results. She was eager to see how the pictures would come out. Two weeks later, not having received the proofs, she called the company. "Ma'am, your rolls came back empty. Did you forget to remove your lens cover." She knew she hadn't, as the camera would show her when the lens was covered, but she had no recourse for regaining her films.

Two years later she went back, while her children were staying with their father. Her mother came along. Again Marika climbed onto the plateau above Gran Pueblo, early in the morning. After shooting two rolls of black and white this time, she stayed for an hour above the ruins, contemplating them. Again she thought she had been there before. At once she had a vision: could she have been a young man working on a well that bubbled up, right into the center of the compound, on the edge of a large kiva, many years ago? She saw herself laying the rocks in a circle with just enough mud to settle them in place. A pole ladder inside the well was placed against the wall. Another young man was feeding him rocks and thick mud in a bucket hanging from a tripod. When the vision faded and Marika had climbed down below the cliffs, she went to look at the spot where she had seen the well. But there was no sign of anything at all, just dirt, no rocks, no vegetation.

She went to have lunch with her mother. The next day as they were leaving the complex, she felt that she was leaving a piece of herself behind. She dropped off the rolls of negatives at a big photo shop in Albuquerque. Three weeks later when she called, she was told that they could not find the negatives or her name in their files. They never gave her a receipt.

    Her next time at Gran Pueblo, Marika went with her father and one of her sisters. This ancient site kept calling her back. She wanted her family to experience it too. In the morning, she and her sister climbed above the pueblo, this time going through a crevasse in the cliffs, instead of hiking around to the top of the plateau. She took one roll of black and white and one roll of color. Again, she felt that she had been here when water was flowing in the canyon in front of the pueblo. She could almost hear people singing, or was it just the wind whistling through the rocks? The three of them went to other smaller sites that had easier access. Her father told her that he had dreamed of that place, many years before. He was grateful to have actually seen this magical site. Then, they went to visit other archeological monuments around the Four Corners. All the rolls of film taken during this trip were given to a reputable photographer near where she lived, and all came back fully developed. At last, Marika was able to make a collage with the pictures of Gran Pueblo.

    The fifth and last time she went there, her partner, her eldest son and his family came with her. Her young granddaughter was very interested at first, but later, she didn't want to go into certain rooms. Marika, once more, took a hundred pictures, this time with a new camera, one with a card that could be downloaded directly onto her computer. After going home with her parents, her very sensitive granddaughter told them how she had liked seeing Gran Pueblo, but never wanted to go back.

When Marika entered the pictures onto her laptop, one of them was very different from the rest. Fragmented multi-colored tiny particles were superimposed on the stone rooms, like a sky-to-earth dotted rainbow. That picture was the very last one she captured of the big pueblo, thinking that it would not be a very good one, but one she somehow needed to take. There had not been a rainbow on that wall when she took its picture, only different shades of sandstone rocks under a clear blue sky. She remembered being alone in front of one door in the wall, spending a long time reflecting about the extensive work involved in building such an immense complex, on the logistics of carrying rocks and timber for it, and wondering why the people who had spent so much time on this sacred place had disappeared all at once. She had cried then, without knowing why.

She showed the picture to two friends with psychic abilities. The first woman said the spirits of hundreds of people were released on the day the picture was taken. A few hours later, the second woman, who had not met with the first one, told her that she had released many souls trapped in the Pueblo. Marika did not know what to think of all this. Whose spirits? Why her? Why at that particular wall? Was it just a trick of the light?

That evening, Marika was still wondering why she could not put the photo out of her mind. In the middle of the night, she had a strange dream.

It had happened many hundred years before. The whole area in and around the Gran Pueblo had dried up. The river had not flowed for as long as many generations remembered. The wells were dry. The precious morning dew was collected every morning. Larger amounts of water had to be carried in from a long distance. Without water, they could no longer raise small livestock. The small gardens of herbs, corn, beans and squash depended on the paltry monsoons, and they did not produce enough to last till the next growing season. There was a lot of sickness. She was a mid-wife and a healer. Her name was Maia. It was torture to see the pain and misery the people suffered. The women were having difficulties birthing. So many of the babies were born dead.

The wonderful aura of sharing, caring, participating in ceremonies that were the culmination of the spiritual community of all the local tribes, had deteriorated in the last decades. It was gone, evaporated, like the memory of moisture when a dark cloud hovers above but never rains. There were no longer any of the traditional celebrations. The other tribes nearby were not welcome anymore.

Instead of equality amongst all, a tyrant, a tall, wide, muscular man, was ruling the whole complex, with an uncompromising will. Upon his arrival, many years before, he had declared himself to be a shaman directly descended from Quetzalcóatl, the feathered serpent god of the Toltecs. He ruled like a dictator, asking for remuneration in the form of food, tools, precious stones, skins, feathers, and young human blood. It was rumored that he would eat the heart, liver and brain of the ones who were sacrificed, and then their flesh would be hung and dried, and given to those that were hungry. He was feared by all around him. He claimed to know that enemies were coming from far away lands to invade and plunder the towns, and that he was providing protection to all his followers. Yet fear, famine and sickness prevailed, while he pranced around the town, wearing a large serpent mask with long multicolored feathers surrounding it and a plastron made of polished, golden metal leaves.

She was trying her best to help her people. Maia did not believe in anything the tyrant was offering, and he reviled her in return, claiming her to be a fraud as a healer. He would criticize her for the loss of anyone who died of thirst, or hunger, or accident, especially if they were under her care. But no one dared challenge the human sacrifices he made for appeasing the gods. The old curandera she had acquired her knowledge from had warned her about him. But she had died mysteriously while Maia was still young. Being the oldest apprentice, Maia took over her medicine practice at the Gran Pueblo.

Immediately after she moved there, the

self-appointed ruler had tried to forcefully seduce her, but she had been able to ward him off with her will, spells and amulets. The huge man repulsed her. He certainly did not belong to any tribe she knew. He was big-boned, hairy like an animal. Despite his tan, his skin was lighter than everyone else. Above his hands that were tattooed black, the inside of his forearms were very pale. He wore his mask all the time, although it made him sweat during the warm summer months. She had seen him up close, seen his neck covered with short curly red hair. Under the mask, she had glimpsed hair on his face. But the worst was the awful smell exuding from him, like an old beast whose insides were rotting.

One day, Maia was helping one of his concubine give birth. But the baby was early and came out very deformed. Parts of his limbs were missing, a hole gaped in the middle of his chest where his insides were showing. She could not get his breath to start until many minutes after delivery. His whole body was blue at first, and finally turned light purple shortly before he died. She brewed a strong tea to stop the mother's bleeding and showed her how to hold pressure on her womb to stop the flow. Maia told her she would take the little child and follow the old traditions to send him into the next world. But the malevolent dictator had come in and said: "You will do no such thing. You killed my son. Now you will die for it." While she was holding the baby, he pulled out a sharp pointed blade and quickly pierced both her eyes. He was so strong, she could not fend him off. As blood ran down her face, his woman cried out. The demon grabbed Maia by her long braid and dragged her outside, to the middle of the great square, and tossed her in a dried-up well. "Here," he said. "If you have any power, fill this well with water."

She broke her arm in the fall as she crumpled to the bottom. She tried to climb out of the pit, but it was too steep. She could not see what she was doing. She could not get a hold on the rocks, with her useless arm. No one dared help her, so great was the fear of provoking the big man. She sunk back to the ground and prayed to all the gods she knew to release her people from the darkness that surrounded them. She named aloud all the children, women and men who had departed life during her time, sending them to better places. When she was done, she started naming everyone all over again.

The next morning, she heard many people cry, imploring the tyrant. The loudest voice in the forefront she recognized as Otseha. She had trained Otseha since she was a child, teaching her all she knew about helping others. When ready, Otseha had gone to the next village on the rising sun side, and was practicing there. As soon as she heard about Maia's troubles, she had rushed to her aid. Once she arrived at the pit, she asked for ropes. No one came forward to help. She tossed Maia a skin of water. Maia drank a few sips to heal her parched throat.

She told Otseha to run, to go back to her village as she was afraid for her, for she was known for being her apprentice and her friend. But the young healer would not leave, and asked again for ropes or cloth that would help her remove Maia from the well. Most of the people stood back. A few ran to their rooms to get long poles and sisal ropes.

Before help came back in time, the malevolent ruler heard about Otseha's whereabouts. As usual he wore the feathered snake mask, his chest shield, a long knife and a large stone hammer. The crowd parted in front of him. Many started crying. Otseha stared at him and howled in anger. The vile ogre stopped her wailing by breaking her neck. Then he tossed her in the old well, like trash, and told the masses to go back to work. He placed two of his feared guards near the pit, with orders to kill and throw in anyone coming to help. Then he ordered a few men to gather as much dirt as they could carry in a skin, and toss it into the pit until it was full.

Maia held her friend tight, after straightening her head so that her spirit would travel unimpeded to her next life. She cried as clumps of earth were thrown into the pit, until she could no longer breathe.

Marika woke up with a start, drenched in sweat. This had seemed so real. Was she there at one time? No one knows what had really happened at Gran Pueblo. Why did they all leave at once, many centuries ago? The elders are not talking. Do they even know? All the rumors passed on are conjectures.

Only the whispering spirits in the cliffs of this extraordinary land know the truth.

~~~

A Division of Two

Dear Rhonda,

This is the last time I use you for my personal schemes, the very last letter I will force you to write, the very last intrusion into your senses. Now that you have discovered my transcendent persona, I am moving on to new realms.

I remember when I first met you on your thirteenth birthday. Your least favorite school mate, Martha, whom you were obliged to invite to your party, had hacked off your cake into irregular pieces, handing you the ugliest chunk of it all. I made you roar in rage. I made you slap that cake in her face. I made you kick everyone out. I alleviated the guilt of your past suffering.

And your first boyfriend, Jonas, who wanted you to do unspeakable things to him, that you almost choked to death after threatening to cut off his manhood. I was the one guiding you, that day.

And that time, after you graduated, you got into your new, used car and ran over the nasty neighbors' dog who always barked at you for no reason. That neighbor, who looked like your uncle, had screamed at you when you got back home. You had vociferated curses at him until he retreated to his house. He never spoke to you again, nor obtained another dog.

And your father, who had invited his brother to your wedding, a year after you had met sweet James, the only person who would forgive all your maleficences. I made you retch your breakfast on your father's expensive, new suit, and yell at him for having such a destitute, inconsiderate, inbred family, and then cancel the nuptials.

Not to forget your mother, who would find you the most appalling employments, and would even drive you to the interviews. She had always managed to close her eyes upon any harm inflicted to you. But I made sure your foulmouth and your indecent demeanor during those interrogations destroyed any hopes she had of getting you out of her house.

But then you met Sonia. She did not mind your switch of temper, your transition from the older docile, timid and virtuous you to the new hostile, violent and impudent me. She saw right through my attachment to you. She helped you discover the obscene pain inflicted to your immature body by your uncle. She prompted you to forgive this uncle for his abuse, to forgive yourself for suffering this assault, to forgive your family and your friends for their ignorance, and finally to forgive me for taking over your soul.

I thank you for letting me occupy your body

for all these years, for liberating me, for releasing my spirit to seek a next path and for teaching me compassion.

May the rest of your current life be peaceful and filled with the happiness you deserve,
> Your Departing Attachment

Three Stone Masons

Juan Doe was contemplating the blank wall behind Dr. Eduardo Ramirez. That was all he had been doing since arriving at the mental hospital four months before. Totally naked, squatting on the large armchair in the doctor's office, with his arms tightly wrapped around his legs, toes curled around the edge of the seat, he was just staring straight ahead, not acknowledging the doctor's presence.

At night, the overhead camera in his room showed him straightening himself, stretching his limbs, before going to sleep on the blanket he had laid directly on the hard floor. His dreams always seemed to agitate him. The evening he was brought in the hospital, Xavier, the head nurse, had given him the name Juan Doe, knowing it was a racist slur, but from one hispanic to an Indio, he felt justified. Still feeling remorse for the name, the nurse would spend much of the night watching the new addition to the local madness. After a while, he had noticed that a few seconds before someone would come into the room, Doe would curl up into a fetal pose and close his eyes. Each time someone would dress him up, he removed the clothes and shoes with stiff movements, before returning to his cramped posture.

A white man in an old Jeep with Arizona plates had dropped him off, naked and unconscious, in the middle of the main street at Tekapo, a Zuni village in New Mexico. Having tanned brown skin, the locals thought him Amerindian, but definitely not Zuni.

The doctor was baffled by this subject who did not seem to understand English or Spanish or any of the Native American languages of the Four Corner states. At times, when Dr. Ramirez would confront him directly, standing in front of him and talking in a loud voice, Juan would emit deep guttural sounds, tongue clicks or short hissing. Black hair, black eyes, a curved nose on a wide face, he was short and thin with tight muscles and small fine hands. The doctor believed he came from Central America, from some remote tribe. Once, when he thought he was starting to reach him, Juan had sung two short notes in a very high pitched voice, so high that he broke the water glass on the desk. Eduardo Ramirez had been showing him pictures of the sea and of small fishing boats.

The next day, the psychiatrist had brought in a mirror, reflecting the man's face, to which he had made a short clicking sound. Then when he was shown the pictures of the ocean again, he had repeated the high pitch tone and broke the mirror. From his reaction to the pictures, the doctor had deduced that the subject was brought in by boat via the Pacific coast. He also believed that the man could produce something close to an ultrasound. He would have to run some tests to confirm that speculation, even if it meant breaking a few more glasses.

Not having received any definite answers from the naked Indian, besides his reaction to the ocean, he had asked other medics and even practitioners of alternative medicine for their opinions. A hypnotherapist, who was unable to reach the subject orally, had suggested a Native American shaman. To no avail, the psychiatrist had searched for one within the pueblos west of Albuquerque, until a friend had recommended Horse's Eyes, a gifted healer from the Navajo nation in northern Arizona.

~~~

After he was told a little about Juan Doe, including his lack of clothing, Horse's Eyes and his friend had brought with them a narrow cotton cloth, a woven belt and soft moccasins. His companion had put the loin cloth and the supple shoes on the naked man, who had kept both on and purred like a cat.

A ceremony ensued. A cloth decorated with many symbols was placed on the little table in Juan's room. Rocks, crystals, a long red stone pipe, a wooden flute, small boxes filled with powders of different colors and a few other objects were spread upon the cloth. Then, herbs were smoked and other herbs were smudged, sending the smoke detector into a screaming fit. Juan looked up at it and uttered a short high pitch sound and the sensor fell to the ground, silenced. With admiration, Horse's Eyes nodded his head at the stranger.

Dr. Ramirez went to the video camera he had installed on a tripod. He was about to turn it on when an electric shock made him snap his hands off the camera. The camera fell over, breaking the lens in the process. Juan had regained his fetal posture on the floor and had his eyes closed. The shaman barked: "No camera! Maybe you leave the room now." He mad a hand gesture to his helper, who stood up to move the doctor out. But the psychiatrist refused. He told them he would be quiet, just sit and watch, after mentioning that he was paying them and needed to observe the proceedings for his medical evaluation.

Juan started to relax when Horse's Eyes began to sing. His helper beat a steady rhythm on a drum during the whole session. A sweet-smelling bundle of herbs was lit up. Then a clear liquid was sprinkled on Juan, who did not seem to mind. In the corner, the doctor was furiously writing on his pad. The shaman sprinkled some yellow powder first on Juan, then on the cloth. He followed with a coarse blue powder, then with a red one and finally with a very fine white flour. While chanting again, he took a round, white rock and moved it over the man's head, his heart and his lower abdomen. Then the shaman raised a clear crystal up above his head, then near each of his ears, as if listening to what the faceted stone was saying. He picked up a black, round rock and placed it over the same places as the white one. He followed with two more rocks, one red and one yellow. His helper was still striking a steady beat on a narrow drum. At once, the drumming intensified louder and louder. Horse's Eyes blew on his flute a few strident single notes. He raised the crystal high again, then placed it back on the altar. The drumming stopped. A smudge stick was lit up. A large feather was used to aim the smoke all around Juan. The tools were carefully placed back into a wooden box. The drum went inside a backpack. Juan and the shaman were staring at each other, then without words they seemed to reach an agreement. Horse's Eyes turned to the psychiatrist and told him: "This man is a powerful man, who has lost one of his twins. He cannot function in this world without this other part of him." The shaman turned to his helper and they had a heated discussion in their own language. He looked at the doctor. "I will come back in a few days with bigger medicine. I will bring the woman who talks to animals and the man who listens to rocks. Do not bother this man anymore. Give him clean fruits and clean roots to eat." He took the few large dollar bills the doctor gave him and left abruptly.

 On his way to work, Xavier, the night nurse, picked up an assortment of fruits, two carrots, a few jalapeños and a jicama root at the local health food store. He had grown fond of Juan, and was pleased to see that he was getting help from another Native American. The doctor had said clean fruits and roots.

Anything would be better than force-fed overcooked mushy meats and vegetables, followed by green jello, that Juan would spit out like poison. He wouldn't drink milk, but took in a few sips of water on his own from a plastic bottle. Xavier eventually gave him his personal insulated bottle filled with spring water, from which he drank fully.

After checking in on all the other patients, Xavier prepared Juan's dinner. He knew most of the hospital food served earlier would have been rejected by the small man. On a large plastic plate, he placed an apple, a jalapeño, a banana, a piece of jicama and a steamed carrot. He unlocked the door, saw him curled up on his blanket, and set down the plate on the table. The nurse went back to his station and looked at the screen showing Juan's room. After a couple of minutes, he saw him raise his head and stare at the plastic cover hiding the camera in the ceiling. Xavier was surprised he knew he was being watched. Then the thin man walked to the table and slowly ate the banana, the jicama with its skin and the whole hot pepper. He burped, drank some water, stretched and went to lay down on his blanket. He looked once more at the camera above him and closed his eyes.

In the morning, the apple and the carrot were still there. Xavier slipped in a few organic fruits, the rest of the jicama and the raw carrot, before he left at the end of his shift. He asked the day nurse to let him know when and what Juan ate during the day.

Once the hospital workers knew that "Whondo" — a combined form of Juan and wonder as they called him, was now eating in his room, they took an interest in him. They no longer had to put him on a chair, strap him and wheel him to the dining hall, then force-feed him food that he would immediately spit back at them. He was finally eating. They had all been afraid he was starving. And now his door stayed unlocked. The daytime crew would bring him organic, raw fruits and roots that he would sometimes eat in front of them. He would share a tongue click and a short purr for the fruits he liked best.

Whondo had become a pet. Dr. Ramirez officially approved the socialization of the feral man. He himself would spend ten to twenty minutes each day with Juan. He would talk to him loudly in Spanish, still hoping that he understood on some level, and bring him exotic, organic, raw roots. He watched him one day, eat a bitter turmeric root, chewing it with delight, then gently growling while looking straight at him, showing him bright orange teeth as if smiling. The doctor thought it a huge progress in the taming of this wild man.

~~~

It took twelve days for Horse's Eyes to return with more company. The doctor met everyone, but could not remember any of the foreign sounding names. Juan was standing up in a corner. He looked up at the camera, then at the floor. He seemed ready to bolt. The doctor had asked one of the nurses to record the session through the overhead camera. He made a motion for Juan to sit down. The man squatted in a tight position, his back to the wall, and waited in his corner.

The smudge stick smoked up the room. The smoke sensor hadn't been replaced. The older woman with long black hair and even darker eyes, went to Juan, while the shaman set up his altar on the flimsy table. A dwarf man moved close to the small man and folded himself into a ball, his large head turned inward toward his belly. The third new person, a very tall and thin man was standing rigidly straight near the doctor, looking sternly at the group. The drummer was present again. The room was too crowded, too small for all present, Juan retreated further in his corner and closed his eyes.

After a couple of prayers were sung, the woman raised her wrinkled hands as if invoking the sky, before lowering them to her knees as she bent down, her face not too far from Juan, who was watching her intently. In the silence that ensued, they could hear the warbling of various song birds coming from her mouth, then the hoots of water birds seemed to be circulating inside the room. The sound intensified, until the woman was screeching like a bird of prey. She was using the whole gamut of different raptors' sounds, from owls and hawks to vultures. When she made the sound of the golden eagle, Juan got up and clicked his tongue. Then he took the same pose as the woman, facing her, feet planted, legs wide apart and hands on his knees, squawking the same sound alternately with her. After a couple of minutes, she stopped and he retreated to squat in his corner. The dwarf man moved right next to him, his head tilted to one side. The fierce woman looked at Juan again for a while. Then in the charged but quiet room, they heard bears, hyenas, lions, and other felines. Juan got on all fours and growled softly, a deep, low, purring sound that seemed incongruous coming from such a thin body. "A cougar," the old woman quietly said. The short man made a circular gesture ending with both hands in front of him. "He wants more," he said in a gravelly voice. The woman looked again at Juan, but seemed to have run out of sounds. He hissed, then laid down on his belly, elbows up but palms down on the floor. The dwarf man touched Juan's lower back with one hand. He exhaled loudly and said something in his native tongue to the woman, then folded himself again into a ball. The wild-haired woman translated: "He is looking for the gray iguana."

After a couple of quiet minutes, the drumming started, slow and steady. The dwarf unfolded himself and stood above Juan, who had sat up. Moving slowly, he placed his hand on the sitting man's head. Flinching first at the touch, the patient then relaxed as the short man rubbed the top of his head. In his raspy, stammering voice, he said one word

"Xaltachkan". Then with both hands he forced the Juan's head downward. To Dr. Ramirez, it looked like the dwarf was pushing the man's whole body into the floor, until only his dark hair remained visible. This was surreal. The doctor started getting up to check on Juan, but the tall, stern man near him with one hand on his shoulder, drove him back down on his chair.

The large-headed, short man kneeled behind the buried head, and with great effort pulling him first by the hair that seemed the last thing visible above the floor, he lifted Juan's head up out of the ground. The skull elongated until it looked like the cranium of babies pulled out by forceps. Then the two shoulders, followed by the torso appeared above the floor. The drumming became louder. The strong dwarf grabbed Juan by the waist and pulled him up. Finally the legs and feet were out. The doctor rubbed his eyes. This was an illusion. He would see what really happened on the tape, when this crazy farce was over. But he thought Juan Doe's head did seem longer than before, and his face looked wider too, and most importantly, he looked pleased with the whole charade.

The five Indian mystics conferred in a corner, away from the doctor. Juan was lying on his back, his eyes wide open, starring into nothingness. The sadness that had been showing on his face was gone, replaced with a radiant calm.

Horse's Eyes blew into his flute. A few sharp notes on a simple rhythm. Over and over again. The steady beat on the drum had started also when the flute did. The doctor thought that they were all being mesmerized by sounds, which was what must have made him hallucinate.

Horse's Eyes moved towards Juan, who was still lying prone on his blanket. With a long yucca stick, he touched the top of his head, while blowing a single note. The small man's whole body shook. Then the shaman touched his heart. Juan shook again. But when he tapped on his stomach, the small man did not flinch. A large, clear crystal was placed on his groin. As they all watched, the rock's inner light dulled. A web of cracks appeared on its surface as it darkened further. The Shaman quickly removed the crystal and blew sage smoke on it. After the crystal had regained its clarity, he chanted the same phrase a few times, in his native tongue. The drumming stopped.

The five shamans, standing in a circle with their heads tilted inward, discussed quietly together. Ramirez could not understand a word of it. The rigid man turned to him and spoke in English, "They are triplets, born from the same pod. The iguana is caught inside the new spider's web. Xaltachkan must find and release Iguana to become whole again."

"Can you explain this to me? What does this mean?" Dr. Ramirez asked. The tall man looked at him as if he was stupid. "The claws of Iguana unearth the rock. The voice of Cougar shapes the rock. The eyes of Eagle transport the rock." Sensing that the doctor still didn't understand, he continued:

"Xaltachkan came from very long ago, before the great water's time. We now live in the wind's time. Xaltachkan waits for the long portal to come back so they can build temples again on sacred grounds. That time is coming soon, but without Iguana, the correct building rocks cannot be found. "

Eduardo Ramirez was still not grasping what this meant for his patient. Pointing at Juan, with a tone of incredibility he asked: "Is he this Xaltachkan?" The rigid man stiffly answered in a deep slow tone, as if scolding a child. "You must respect Xaltachkan. They are two out of three, this day. The new spider has trapped the third one of them. They cannot find, cut or move the stones until they are three again. The new spider has woven a toxic web all over our material world. The animals, the people, the plants, all have been captured in his web. Everything on the earth is crippled. The new spider has trapped Iguana, the earth element, to bring more darkness and division amongst all the earth's creatures." As if having said too much, he turned around and got ready to leave.

Xavier burst into the room as the five Navajos were reaching the door. He had come in early. As asked, another nurse had called him when the shamans had shown up. He had been unable to watch anything on his monitor, but heard the whole conversation through a microphone in the room. "Good afternoon, Honored Sir," addressing himself to the tall man who was leading the pack. "Can you tell me where the iguana is trapped, please? I would like to help Xaltachkan find it." The taller Navajo who had been interpreting for the others, softened up and replied, "Iguana is trapped under volcanic rocks, in what you call El Malpais, east of the sacred lands of the Zunis and of the Ramah. When you go to these lands, you must leave all the electronic toys behind, so the new spider cannot find Xaltachkan. Horse's Eyes will give you protection for the journey. Walk in beauty."

Once the Indian shamans had left the hospital, Dr. Ramirez went to look at the recording. One nurse had started the recording when everyone came into the room. Shortly after the introductions, Juan had looked up at the camera, and the screen had gone blank. The doctor was so frustrated, he screamed at the monitor, he screamed at the nurse who thought he had followed his orders to the letter. Then, having chased everyone from the room, he screamed for a few more minutes at the multiple monitors.

A few minutes later, Xavier knocked on the office door and gave his leave of absence to the doctor.

"How long will you be gone for?"

The nurse replied, "I have over thirty days of unused personnel time. If I need more, I will let you know. Or I can quit! Please, sign Juan out. I'll take good care of him. We're going to El Malpais, to find what he has lost."

The camera was working again. They both looked at what Juan was doing. He was putting the moccasins on.

Ramirez said: "He's leaving right now, isn't he?" He agreed to sign Juan over to Xavier's care. After all, no one had claimed him in four months, and the state was only paying part of his hospital bill.

He asked Xavier to come back when he was done, and to let him know what happened and how Juan fared. The big nurse was his best mental health attendant, and good medics were hard to find, especially for night shifts. He would miss him if he left for long.

As Xavier reached Juan's room, the little man was at the open door, looking both ways at the corridor in front of him. The nurse covered him with his lab coat and took him home.

~~~

The car ride was stressful for Xaltachkan. He squatted on the seat and kept trying to pull off the safety belt. When they arrived inside the garage, Juan became nervous again and wanted to run outside. Xavier led him into the kitchen and prepared him a bowl of fresh fruits. After they ate, he took him to the spare bedroom. He patted the bed to invite him to it, but Juan just stood still by the door.

How was he going to reach this man? His mother had been somewhat psychic while she was alive. She used to touch foreheads with him and transmit emotions that way. Calmly, with one hand Xavier touched the man's head, then he bent his forehead to his. He tried to transmit mentally to the wild man, "I will not harm you. I will not harm you. I want to help you find the iguana. We can go to the volcanic lands tomorrow morning." Juan clicked his tongue. He took off the lab coat he was still wearing, stretched his arms and legs, and laid down on the small rug next to the bed. Then he closed his eyes and seemed to fall asleep.

Xavier still had the first vehicle he ever owned. An old four-wheel drive, three-quarter ton, Ford pick-up he had bought used, while going to nursing school. He kept it in good running condition, only used it to transport heavy loads. He thought the truck would have less 'electronic toys' as the shaman had said, than the modern commuter car he normally used.

The next morning, after they passed through Grants, they took the western road to the badlands, going toward the Ramah and the Zuni Reservations. Once they got to the edge of the national monument, Xavier stopped at every dirt road and trail head going into the park. They no longer needed to touch their foreheads to communicate. Xavier would look into Juan's eyes and they were able to exchange simple thoughts and sometimes pictures, like the grey iguana, into each other's mind. But Juan did not want to search any of the first trails. As they got to the western edge of the park, Juan pointed south with his hand parallel to the ground. Xavier took the first dirt road going south. Soon they were surrounded by lava rocks on all sides. They drove a little further and Juan pointed east, another two-track trail leading toward the center of the park. A few feet near the end of the trail, the truck stalled and would not start again. Only sharp dark red and brown rocks surrounded them.

Juan purred, his nostrils flared up. "Iguana is here."

From behind the seat, Xavier got two backpacks containing fruit, bottles of water and flashlights. But Juan took one of the bottles and refused the rest. "Light, to see in the dark," Xavier transmitted. Juan flashed back in his mind a picture of a night vision of a lava tube. It was like looking through the night goggles the big nurse had learned to use during his time as a military helicopter paramedic. He saw the head of a cougar imprinted on Juan's head. He remembered. Three in one: the eagle, the cougar, the iguana. The cougar could see in the dark. Juan would not need any light.

Xaltachkan climbed down into a rugged sink hole. On one side, a large lava tube gaped open. Xavier prepared himself to follow, but the small man turned around and stopped him. He transferred his thoughts, "Iguana is near. We will go to him. You go back. Your way is good!" He turned and disappeared into the darkness of the lava tube. "I will wait for you," Xavier shouted at his back.

He waited for a whole long day, eating fruits and canned foods, drinking most of the water, sleeping on the bench seat. Early on the second day, thinking he may have missed him coming out at night, he walked to the sink hole. He dropped into the dark lava tube, but could not see or hear anything. He called him a few times, the tunnel echoed pointlessly.

The truck started right up. It must have gotten hot the day before, while moving slowly on the dirt roads. He went to the visitor center and asked for a Search and Rescue team. A couple of hours later, the search teams showed up. Two dog teams with them. The handlers put leather booties on their dogs. "The lava will cut their paws," they explained. Xavier only had the lab coat as a scent article for Juan. Although it had his own odor as well as the feral man's, it seemed to be enough for the dogs. They both signaled at the head of the lava tube.

Two Ramah Navajo men came along. They told Xavier that no one had ever come out of this particular lava tube. It plunged deep into the earth. It belonged to the spirit world. Only bats, scorpions and spiders lived in it.

One of the dog teams led the way and entered the tube followed by foot teams with heavy backpacks. The other dog team searched around the perimeter of the hole. Xavier was very worried. Two days without food, and probably running out of water, his moccasins would be cut to shreds by now, and how far down did this tube go anyhow?

Just before dark, the teams emerged. All the searchers were coughing, gagging and rubbing their eyes. The dog also seemed exhausted. The radios had not worked down in the tube, so the teams had been unable to report anything. They handed Xavier the bottle he had given Juan. It seemed full. The team leader explained that they had gotten to the very end of the tunnel, where the wall had collapsed a long time ago. No side tunnels, only the same tube to the end, plunging deep into the ground. No signs of anyone but this bottle of water, right where it had caved in. Xavier thanked them and told them that he would stay one more day in the area in case his friend showed up.

He climbed into his car, getting ready for another uncomfortable night on the truck's seat. But first, he opened Juan's bottle of water to get a drink. Something seemed to be moving inside it. He shone his flashlight inside the bottle. An image of an eagle, a cougar and an iguana fused together was reflected in the water. He looked again. All three were still there. He closed the bottle, hoping the vision would not fade. The Xaltachkan were reunited. "May your way be good!" he voiced aloud to the lava tube, just before he left.

~~~

Dreams are prompted by the subconscious.

Reincarnation is the rejuvenation of the soul in a material body.

A traumatic past life can resurface in a young person's soul.

A dire past may manifest as a presence.

Dreams of reincarnation can assist in revealing a mystery.

One entity may attach to a corporeal body.

The soul is eternal.